Best Loved Stories from
CHARLES DICKENS

INTRODUCTION

Charles Dickens was born on February 7th 1812 in Portsmouth, England, the second of eight children. John Dickens, his father, was a clerk in the Navy Pay Office.

During his childhood, Charles moved house a number of times. In 1817, the Dickens family went to London, but all did not go well there. In 1824, John Dickens was imprisoned for debt in Marshalsea Prison. At the age of twelve, Charles went to work in a blacking factory, earning six shillings a week. It was an experience that contributed greatly to his later views on social reform.

Once his father was free, Charles attended Wellington House Academy, then joined a legal firm before becoming a journalist for the *Morning Chronicle*. In 1836, he married Catherine Hogarth. Already he was more than a reporter. *Sketches by Boz* (1836–37) was followed by the serialization of *The Pickwick Papers*. Then came *Oliver Twist* and *Nicholas Nickleby*. In all he wrote fifteen major novels and countless short stories and articles. As well as writing, he enjoyed travel and amateur theatricals. His marriage ended in 1858. It had not been a happy affair but did produce ten children.

Charles Dickens died at Gad's Hill near Rochester, Kent, on June 9th 1870, aged only 58. He is buried in Poet's Corner in Westminster Abbey. The inscription on his tombstone says, "He was a sympathiser to the poor, the suffering, and the oppressed; and by his death, one of England's greatest writers is lost to the world."

Best Loved Stories from
CHARLES DICKENS

Retold by
SUE BUTLER

Illustrated by
JENNY THORNE

ARMADILLO

Published by Armadillo Books
an imprint of
Bookmart Limited
Registered Number 2372865
Trading as Bookmart Limited
Desford Road
Enderby
Leicester
LE19 4AD

ISBN 1-84322-012-1

Produced for Bookmart Limited by Nicola Baxter
PO Box 215
Framingham Earl
Norwich Norfolk NR14 7UR

Designer: Amanda Hawkes
Production designer: Amy Barton

Printed in Singapore

CONTENTS

THE WORKS OF CHARLES DICKENS

A
CHRISTMAS
CAROL

Nobody ever stopped Ebenezer Scrooge in the street to say, "My dear Scrooge, how are you?" He was a cold-hearted, grasping, solitary old man, with a shrivelled, sharp face and no love for his fellow men.

Fog swirled frequently through the streets of Victorian London. It was thickened by the smoke from thousands of coal fires—the only means of cooking and heating for most people.

One Christmas Eve, Scrooge was busy in his counting-house. Outside, it was bitter, foggy weather. At three o'clock, it was already dark, and the miser worked by candlelight, keeping an eye on his clerk in a tiny room next door.

Scrooge wasn't feeling at all festive. When his nephew came in, red-cheeked from the cold, to wish him a merry Christmas, the miser made a sour face. "Bah! Humbug! Every idiot who goes about with 'Merry Christmas' on his lips should be boiled with his own pudding!" he replied, sending the young man on his way.

At last it was time to finish business for the day. As Bob Cratchit, his poor clerk, scuttled home for his only day of holiday in the year, Scrooge returned to his dark, depressing lodgings. It was so dark that he had to grope his way to his front door.

Suddenly, to his horror, the door-knocker seemed to turn into a horrible, ghostly face— the face of his dead business partner Jacob Marley. It was only for a moment, but Scrooge was badly shaken. He checked carefully through all his rooms by candlelight before he at last sat down by a feeble fire.

But as Scrooge crouched near the embers, he heard a ghastly clanking sound from the cellars below. It sounded as if a heavy chain was being dragged across the floor. It came closer ... and closer.

It was the ghost of Jacob Marley, complete with pigtail, waistcoat, tights and boots. The chain he dragged was long and made of cash boxes, keys, padlocks, ledgers, deeds and heavy purses wrought in steel.

Sitting down, Marley told Scrooge, "I wear the chain I forged in life." Scrooge was loath to trust his senses. "A slight disorder of the stomach makes them cheats," he told the ghost. "You may be an undigested bit of beef, a blot of mustard...."

But Marley really was a ghost and because in his lifetime he never wandered far beyond the counting-house, he must now travel constantly, unable to rest. Before leaving, he warned Scrooge to expect three spirits, because the miser still had a hope and chance of escaping Marley's fate. The ghost went to the window, and Scrooge saw the air filled with phantoms wandering around in restless haste.

Shocked and exhausted, Scrooge fell into bed fully clothed.

Although it was after two in the morning when he went to bed, Scrooge awoke to hear the neighbouring church clock striking midnight. He rubbed frost from the window and peered into the foggy darkness.

Scrooge went back to bed. Time slowly passed. When the bell struck a dull, deep, hollow, melancholy *one*, the curtains of the bed were swept back and a strange figure appeared—like a child but also like an old man. His hair was white, but his face had no wrinkles. From the crown of his head shone a bright, clear jet of light. In a gentle voice he said, "I am the Ghost of Christmas Past."

*Before wristwatches were worn, and when only the wealthy could afford pocket watches, the **church clock** was an important timekeeper for ordinary people.*

Holding the ghost's hand, Scrooge passed through a wall and found himself back in the place where he grew up. Boys on ponies were leaving school for Christmas. Scrooge wept to see himself left alone and forgotten in the school-room.

Then the ghost showed him another Christmas. Scrooge saw a little girl—his sister Fan. She was a delightful child, big-hearted and full of life, but she died as a young woman, leaving a son, Scrooge's nephew Fred.

Next the ghost took Scrooge to the warehouse where he was apprenticed and showed him Mr. Fezziwig, in his French wig, sending Scrooge and Dick Wilkins to clear a space for the Christmas dance. There was a fiddler, meat and cake, mince pies and beer. Scrooge saw his young self and Dick pouring out their hearts in praise of Mr. Fezziwig.

Then the ghost showed Scrooge himself as an older man, without the harsh and rigid lines of later years but already with the signs of greed and avarice on his face. He saw a pretty girl in mourning dress releasing him from his engagement, an agreement made when they were both content to be poor.

Scrooge begged not to be shown more, but the ghost held his arms and forced him to see the girl, grown into a woman, surrounded by happy, boisterous children. Scrooge tried to smother the ghost, but his light would not be extinguished.

Scrooge fell asleep again but awoke suddenly to hear the church bell once again striking *one*. No ghost appeared, but there was a blaze of ruddy light coming from the next room. Scrooge entered to find it hung with holly, mistletoe and ivy. Heaped up to form a throne were pheasants, suckling pigs, apples, oranges, cake and bowls of punch. On the throne sat a jolly giant, wearing a green robe edged with white fur. He was the Ghost of Christmas Present.

The ghost showed Scrooge people getting ready to enjoy Christmas. Together, the ghost and Scrooge travelled to the home of Bob Cratchit and saw him returning from church with his son, the lame Tiny Tim, on his shoulders. Goose and a rather small pudding was enjoyed, then the whole family sat by the fire and ate chestnuts.

Scrooge was shown Christmas in a mining village, in a lighthouse and on a ship— even in his nephew's house. Then the ghost began to age and brought forth a boy and a girl, yellow, meagre, ragged and scowling, named Want and Ignorance.

As the clock struck twelve, all this disappeared, but when Scrooge looked up, a phantom wearing a long black robe appeared. He was the Ghost of Christmas Yet To Come.

This ghost showed Scrooge some businessmen discussing a man's funeral, which would be cheap, as few people would want to attend. Scrooge looked hard but could not see himself among the men.

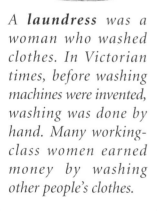

*A **laundress** was a woman who washed clothes. In Victorian times, before washing machines were invented, washing was done by hand. Many working-class women earned money by washing other people's clothes.*

The ghost then took him to a part of town that was steeped in filth, crime and misery. Here a grey-haired rascal met a charwoman, a laundress and an undertaker, who all had goods to sell, stolen from the dead man. Scrooge was shown a body laid out on a bed, but the face was covered. Scrooge asked the ghost if anyone felt any emotion at this man's death. The ghost showed him Bob Cratchit's house, where Bob's wife's first reaction was to be happy at the news. Later Scrooge was shown the Cratchit family again. This time the family was upset but trying to be brave, for Tiny Tim had died.

Scrooge asked to know the name of the mysterious dead man whom no one mourned. The ghost took him to a graveyard and showed him a gravestone. The graveyard was horrible, walled in by houses and overrun with grass and weeds.

Before approaching the stone, Scrooge asked, "Are these the shadows of the things that Will be, or are they shadows of things that May be, only?" The ghost replied that bad deeds lead to bad ends, but people can change if they choose.

Going nearer to the grave, Scrooge saw his own name carved on the stone. Terrified, he promised to honour Christmas in his heart and to try to keep its ideals alive all year. As Scrooge held up his hands in a final prayer to ask for his fate to be reversed, he saw the ghost begin to change shape. It shrank, collapsed and dwindled down into a bed post. Scrooge awoke in his own bed.

Scrooge dressed quickly, and, confused about what day it was, threw open the window. He called to a boy, "What's today my fine fellow?" "Why, CHRISTMAS DAY!" the boy replied, and Scrooge realized that the ghosts had done their work in a single night.

Chuckling, he sent the surprised boy to buy a prize turkey for Bob Cratchit. Then Scrooge dressed and went out. In the street, he met a gentleman who had once asked him in vain for money for the poor. Scrooge begged forgiveness and whispered how much he would like to give, adding "a great many back payments are included in it".

When he arrived at his nephew's for Christmas lunch, Scrooge was surprised to find himself welcomed warmly.

The next day, when Scrooge started to be nice to his clerk, Bob Cratchit was tempted to call for help and a strait-jacket. But Scrooge had really changed, saying warmly, "I'll raise your salary and endeavour to assist your struggling family, and we will discuss your affairs this very afternoon." The ghosts had done their work indeed.

GREAT EXPECTATIONS

My father's family name was Pirrip, and my Christian name Philip. However, all my infant tongue could manage was Pip—and so I came to be called. I never saw my father or my mother. The shape of the letters on my father's tombstone gave me the idea that he was a square, stout man. I imagined my mother freckled and sickly. Ours was marsh country, a dark flat wilderness, near a river and close to the sea.

On a bleak Christmas Eve, I was visiting the graveyard and beginning to cry when a terrible voice cried, "Hold your noise!" and a man started up from between the gravestones. He was a terrible sight, all in coarse grey, with a great iron on his leg.

"You get me a file," he snarled, "and you get me wittles." He ordered me to bring them to the old Battery, early the next morning. "Or I'll have your heart and liver out," he growled.

Leg irons were often used to restrain prisoners in Victorian times. Convicts were treated very harshly, and it was not uncommon for them to have their legs and arms shackled with rings of iron.

I ran without stopping to the forge where I lived with my sister and her husband, the blacksmith Joe Gargery. My sister was tall and bony and always wore a coarse apron. Joe was a sweet-tempered, foolish fellow. Wracked with fear, I could only pretend to eat my supper before going up to bed.

Early next morning, I crept downstairs and took from the pantry bread, cheese, mincemeat, brandy and a handsome pork pie. I stole a file from the forge and ran across the marshes towards the old Battery.

On my way, I observed a man dressed in grey, also with a leg iron, but he quickly vanished. After delivering my stolen goods, I returned home to find visitors arriving for Christmas lunch. There were Mr. Hubble the wheelwright and his wife; Mr. Wopsle the church clerk, and Joe's uncle, called Mr. Pumblechook, a wealthy corn-chandler. I ate in terror of my thefts being noticed.

Then my sister went to get the pork pie.

I left the table and ran to the door—straight into a soldier who held out a pair of broken handcuffs, saying, "Here you are, look sharp."

Joe lit his forge and mended the handcuffs. Then he took me on his back to follow the soldiers. Mr. Wopsle also came, and after a chase, two escaped convicts were recaptured.

One was the man from the graveyard and one was the man who had vanished so suddenly. Recognizing me, the convict from the graveyard said, "I took some wittles ... from the blacksmith's ... liquor and a pie."

I watched as the soldiers rowed the captured men out to the waiting hulks. Soon after, I was summoned by Miss Havisham to play with her adopted daughter Estella. Mr. Pumblechook took me to Satis House, which was a dismal place. We rang the bell and soon a beautiful young lady appeared. Though about my age, she was as scornful and self-possessed as if she had been twenty-one and a queen.

Hulks were prison ships, made in the hulls of large, unwieldy vessels. Moored off the coast in desolate places, they made a forbidding sight.

She led me through the house, which was devoid of daylight. In a room lit by candles, I met Miss Havisham, sitting by a large dressing table. She was dressed as if for a wedding, in white satin, expensive lace and silk, all turned yellow with age. But she had not quite finished dressing. She wore only one shoe. Her gloves and some jewels lay on the dressing table.

For eight months, I visited Satis House, being taunted by Estella, who taught me how common I was. On Miss Havisham's birthday, I met a burly gentleman of dark complexion, who smelled of soap and wore a large watch-chain.

Miss Havisham showed me a room with a table laid for a wedding feast. Everything was thick with dust, and the mouldy cake was hung with cobwebs. She said, "I will be laid here when I am dead."

Later, a pale young man appeared and asked me to fight. Unwillingly, I agreed and knocked him down.

Eventually Miss Havisham gave me twenty-five guineas and I went to work with Joe and his journeyman Dolge Orlick. I no longer visited Satis House.

Then, one fateful day, my sister was attacked when alone in the house. A tremendous blow to the back of her head sent her out of her wits. Thankfully a neighbour, Biddy, came to tend her.

I was in the fourth year of my apprenticeship when I was approached in the tavern by a lawyer, Mr. Jaggers, the burly gentleman I had met at Miss Havisham's house. It seemed that I had come into "great expectations", however, he said, "the name of the person who is your liberal benefactor is to remain a profound secret until the person chooses to reveal it."

*An **apprentice** was a young person being trained by a skilled craftsperson, while a **journeyman** was a craftsman or artisan qualified to work competently at his trade but only under the supervision of an experienced employer.*

I was sure the person must be Miss Havisham. I travelled to London, where I was taken by Wemmick, Mr. Jagger's clerk, to Barnard's Inn. Here I lodged with Herbert Pocket, the son of Miss Havisham's brother Matthew. And here I met again the pale youth with whom I had fought.

Herbert told me how Miss Havisham inherited a fortune while her half-brother received much less. I also heard how she fell in love with a man who said he would marry her and then didn't. It was rumoured that he was already married.

Herbert took me to his family home, where I met two fellow students. Startop was kind, with a woman's delicacy of feature, but Bentley Drummle was a sulky fellow, rich, idle, proud and suspicious.

I struck up a friendship with Mr. Wemmick, who invited me to his strange, castle-like house to meet his Aged Parent.

Soon after, I had dinner with Mr. Jaggers where, as advised by Wemmick, I closely observed Molly the servant. Later, Joe brought a message from Miss Havisham and, when I went to visit, I found Orlick employed as the gate-keeper. Inside I met Estella, now a woman and even more beautiful.

An envelope edged in black brought serious news: my sister had died the previous Monday.

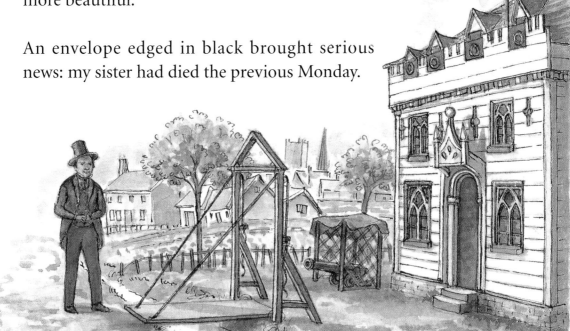

My twenty-first birthday arrived, but my benefactor remained anonymous. I visited Estella at Mrs. Bradley's house in Richmond and found Drummle paying court to her.

Years passed, and I was still living the same wasteful, idle life when one stormy night, I heard a noise. I went to the stair-head and held my reading light over the banister. A man approached, dressed roughly like a seaman. He had long, grey hair and was aged about sixty. It was the convict from the graveyard! I was horror-struck to learn that he was my benefactor, not Miss Havisham.

Sentenced to transportation, he had worked and worked to repay me for getting him food and a file.

"You acted nobly, my boy," he said. "I never forgot it." He told me that the other convict I had met on the marshes was called Compeyson. Before long, Herbert and I realized that Compeyson was the evil trickster who had broken Miss Havisham's heart.

Abel Magwitch, my benefactor, was risking his life by returning from transportation. While he hid, I visited Miss Havisham and her ward. I tried to control my trembling voice as I told Estella, "I have loved you long and dearly."

*In Victorian times, even minor criminals could be sentenced to **transportation**, which meant being taken by boat to Australia. Convicts who returned risked being hanged.*

Estella looked at me unmoved. Miss Havisham had taught her to use her beauty to torture men. When I mentioned Drummle's name, she said haughtily, "I am going to be married to him." I covered my face with my hands.

I arrived at the gate of Barnard's Inn to find a note from Wemmick: "*Do not go home.*" He knew I was being watched.

On Wemmick's advice, Herbert took Magwitch to the house of his fiancée at Mill Pond Bank. Meanwhile, I made plans to get Magwitch on a steamer to Europe. Wemmick also explained how Mr. Jaggers defended Molly his servant, who was charged with murdering another woman. There was a child and a man involved. I remembered how much Mr. Jaggers' servant looked like Estella and was convinced that Molly was Estella's mother.

I visited Miss Havisham. She pleaded with me to forgive her for raising Estelle to have an icy heart, far from her true nature. "Though it be ever so long after my broken heart is dust—pray do it," she begged. I replied, "I can do it now."

Returning from a walk in the garden, I watched the old lady sitting by the fire. Suddenly, a flaming light sprang up, and I saw her running at me, a whirl of fire blazing all around her and soaring above her head. I fought to smother the flames with my coat, then dragged the cloth from the table, scattering the mouldy remains of the wedding feast.

A doctor was called, but it was too late for Miss Havisham. My hands were badly burned, and Herbert took great pains to nurse me. Magwitch was still hiding at Mill Pond Bank, so Herbert and he had talked a great deal about his life. All at once, it became clear to us: Magwitch was Estella's father!

Soon after, I received an anonymous letter, luring me to a little sluice house in the marshes at nine o'clock. It was a trap. I was only saved from being killed by Orlick when Herbert rushed in. Luckily, I had dropped the note and, finding it, he had followed me. Enraged with jealousy, Orlick confessed to killing my sister.

The Thames is a tidal river. In Dickens' day, when many boats were still powered by oars or sails, it was important to know the state of the tide before setting out on a journey

On a March day when the sun shone hot and the wind blew cold, Herbert, Startop and I travelled with Magwitch down the Thames. Herbert and Startop rowed, making good progress with the tide, and we were in position as the steamers approached. Suddenly, a four-oared galley appeared. An official shouted, "You have a returned transport there … I call upon him to surrender." Amongst others in the galley sat Compeyson. A scuffle ensued, during which Compeyson was drowned and Magwitch was severely injured.

Being ill, Magwitch was allowed a chair in court. The sun came in through the great windows as he was sentenced to be hanged.

I made many petitions for clemency but, as the days passed, Magwitch's health deteriorated. One day I held his hand and told him, "you had a child once.... She is living now. She is a lady and very beautiful. And I love her." He died soon after.

I became ill and regained my senses to find myself being tended by Joe. Slowly I grew stronger, but one morning I rose to find Joe had gone. I followed him back to the forge to discover he and Biddy celebrating their wedding day.

There was nothing left for me at home. My fortune was gone and my friends happily settled. I went abroad for eleven years, working as clerk. When I returned, Biddy and Joe had a son.

On a cold afternoon, I visited Satis House, only to find it utterly demolished. In the desolate garden, I beheld a figure.

"Estella!" I cried.

"I am greatly changed," she warned me. But as I took her hand in mine to leave the ruined place, I saw no shadow of another parting from her.

DAVID
COPPERFIELD

I was born at Blundestone, in Suffolk. My father's eyes had closed upon the light of this world six months before mine opened on it.

On a windy March afternoon before my birth, my mother was sitting by the fire, feeling ill and crying, when a strange woman looked in at the window, pressing her nose against the glass. It was my father's aunt, the rich, eccentric Betsey Trotwood.

Though my father had been a favourite of hers, Aunt Betsey had never met my mother—she had disapproved of my father marrying such a "wax doll". Her arrival caused my mother such a shock that I was born that very Friday. However, when the mild doctor, Mr. Chillip, informed Betsey, "It's a boy," she grabbed her bonnet and left without a word.

I was cared for by my mother and the servant Peggotty. With her cheeks and arms so hard and red, I wondered the birds did not peck her in preference to apples. However, the happiness of my childhood was interrupted when Mr. Murdstone began to pay court to my mother.

Barges *were sturdy vessels designed to carry cargo safely. In Victorian times, many trading companies used boats to move goods up and down the coast.*

One day Peggotty took me to visit her family in Yarmouth. I met her brother Daniel and his adopted nephew and niece, Ham and Little Em'ly, who, along with the widow Mrs. Gummage, lived in a large black barge on the beach. It had an iron funnel sticking out for a chimney and a door cut in the side. I quite fell in love with the beautiful Em'ly, who told me as we walked along the beach, "I should like so much to be a lady."

On a cold, grey afternoon, I returned home to find my mother had married Mr. Murdstone. Soon Mr. Murdstone's sister Jane came to live with us, too. Murdstone was a cruel, unfeeling man. One day, when he beat me for not learning my lessons well enough, I caught the hand with which he held me in my mouth and closed my teeth firmly around it. Despite my mother's protestations, I was dispatched to Salem House, a boarding school in London.

Mr. Barkis took me part of the way in his cart, asking me that when I wrote to Peggotty I should give her the strange message, *"Barkis is willin."*

Salem House was run by Mr. Creakle, a friend of cold Mr. Murdstone. On arrival, I found myself forced to wear a sign proclaiming: *Take care of him. He bites.* I would have been miserable had it not been for the good hearted Tommy Traddles and the handsome, confident James Steerforth.

When the holidays arrived, I again travelled with Barkis, who was sad that Peggotty had not responded. You might tell her, he said to me, "Barkis was 'a waitin' for an answer."

It felt strange to be home and discover my mother sitting by the fire, suckling an infant. She and Peggotty kissed me repeatedly. Mr. Murdstone and Jane remained aloof.

I was soon sent back to school, which continued unchanged until the day I was called into Mr. Creakle's office. "Your mother…," he said, "is very … ill … she is … dead."

On my way home, I stopped in Yarmouth to be measured for my mourning clothes. Mr. Omer, the undertaker, was a jolly man, cheerfully assisted by his daughter Minnie and his coffin-maker, called Joram.

Mourning, in Dickens' day, had a formal aspect. It was common to have special black clothes made for it. As a mark of respect, people would often wear black for a year or more after a loved one had died.

Back home, a distraught Peggotty told me, "She was never well for a long time." The baby had also died.

Discharged from service, Peggotty took me to visit Yarmouth again. In a small church, she quietly married the faithful Barkis.

I did not return to school but was sent to the Murdstone & Grinby counting-house in Blackfriars. Here I met Mr. Micawber, who rented me a room. I soon became friends with his wife and children.

*Victorians who fell into debt could be sent to a **debtor's prison**. These were terrible places from which people could only be freed once the debt was paid—an almost impossible task unless the prisoner had wealthy friends to help.*

Mr. Micawber was a stoutish, middle-aged man, with no more hair on his large and shining head than there is upon an egg. He was perpetually in debt and was eventually sent to prison.

On his release, Mr. Micawber decided to leave London with his family. I used guile to get Peggotty to send me money and Aunt Betsy's address in Dover. Though my belongings and money were stolen on the way, I continued my journey on foot, arriving with my clothes and shoes in a woeful condition. Finding my aunt in her neat cottage garden, I announced, "If you please, Aunt, I am your nephew."

"Oh Lord!" said my Aunt, and sat down on the gravel path. But she let me stay, especially after meeting Mr. Murdstone and Miss Murdstone, who rode a donkey across my aunt's beloved green!

I liked living with my strange, eccentric aunt and would often fly a kite with her companion, the child-like Mr. Dick.

One day, my aunt took me to Canterbury. Inside a very old house with long, low, lattice-windows, I met her lawyer, Mr. Wickfield, his dutiful daughter Agnes and his curious-looking clerk Uriah Heep, a high-shouldered, bony youth with red hair cropped like stubble, hardly any eyelashes and no eyebrows.

Waiting for my aunt, I sat opposite the room where Uriah worked. His eyes, like two red suns, observed me stealthily. On Mr. Wickfield's advice, I lodged with him while attending a school run by the kind Dr. Strong.

When I had completed my education, my aunt gave me leave to visit Peggotty while I considered a suitable career. In London I met Steerforth, who took me to Highgate to meet his proud, possessive mother and her companion, Rosa Dartle. Rosa had a scar across her lips. "I was a young boy, and she exasperated me, and I threw a hammer at her," explained Steerforth.

I, in turn, took Steerforth to visit the Peggottys. Ham and Little Em'ly had just become engaged. Steerforth liked Yarmouth so much he bought a boat, so he could sail there regularly.

Back in London once more, I was apprenticed to Spenlow & Jorkins. One evening, I met Agnes, who was visiting London to see her father's agent. She warned me against Steerforth and told me that Uriah was "subtle and watchful. He has mastered Papa's weaknesses," she said, "and taken advantage of them." Talking to me soon after, Uriah confided his passion for Agnes. I was horrified.

But passion was soon to enter my own life. On meeting Mr. Spendlow's silly but beautiful daughter Dora, I fell hopelessly in love. She had the most delightful voice, the gayest laugh, the most fascinating ways. Unfortunately, her father had engaged Miss Murdstone as a companion for his daughter.

One evening, as I was dining with the Micawbers and my old school-friend Tommy Traddles, Steerforth brought a note from Peggotty. Barkis was dying. Naturally, I hurried to Yarmouth.

I was to find that soon after Barkis's death, Em'ly disappeared, leaving Ham a note in which she vowed "never to come back, unless he brings me back a lady." The man involved was Steerforth. Distraught, Peggotty's brother Daniel set off to search for Em'ly, saying, "My unchanged love is with my darling child, and I forgive her."

Back in London, my aunt arrived, claiming that her investments had failed and she and Mr. Dick must live with me. Later, when I visited Canterbury, Agnes revealed that Uriah was now Mr. Wickfield's business partner. No longer a humble clerk, he had moved, with his mother, into the Wickfields' house.

Poor as I was, I had been courting Dora in secret. When Mrs. Murdstone showed my love letters to Dora's father, he vehemently disapproved. However, when he died suddenly, leaving Dora penniless, she was sent to live with her aunts. Eventually, we were married. Beautiful, silly Dora attempted to keep house for me but was totally inept.

On a visit to Canterbury, I found Mr. Micawber working for Uriah, who had virtually taken over the business. I begged Agnes not to marry Uriah just to please her father, who was depressed and drinking heavily.

Back in London once more, I met Daniel Peggotty, newly returned from Europe and still resolutely searching for Em'ly. Later, Steerforth's manservant told me how Steerforth had abandoned Em'ly. Led by Martha to a dingy attic room, Daniel Peggotty at last found his Em'ly. "I thank my Heav'nly Father as my dream's come true," he cried, taking her up in his arms. At once he began to make plans to emigrate to Australia, where Em'ly's past would be unknown.

Dora was gravely ill, but she insisted I go to witness Traddles and Mr. Micawber confronting Uriah. While working for Uriah, Mr. Micawber had discovered how the former clerk had tricked Mr. Wickfield into signing over control of the firm.

Embezzlement is when money or property is entrusted to someone who does not own it, but who fraudulently makes use of it for their own ends.

Uriah had forged Wickfield's signature and framed him for embezzlement. Aunt Betsy waded into the fray, grabbing Uriah, "You know what I want," she shouted. She had feared Mr. Wickfield had embezzled her money but had kept quiet for the sake of Agnes. Now Mr. Wickfield's name was cleared and Aunt Betsy recovered her investments. She kindly lent the Micawbers enough money to make a fresh start in Australia.

Back in London, Agnes was with Dora when she died. Darkness came before my eyes. It felt as if my whole world had ended.

I agreed to take a letter from Em'ly to Ham, but arrived in Yarmouth to find a storm raging and a schooner about to be wrecked on the beach. Unconcerned for his own life, Ham waded into the waves and died attempting to save a stranger, who also died. The stranger was Steerforth.

A **schooner** is a sailing vessel with two masts or more. They were used to transport goods such as fruit from Portugal and sherry from Spain.

The Micawbers and the Peggottys, including Mrs. Gummage and Martha, set sail for Australia. I spent some time in Switzerland, writing about my experiences. I often thought about Agnes, too.

At last, I returned to Dover, where my aunt gave me news of all my old friends and told me she suspected Agnes had an attachment. I called on Agnes and, as we spoke of Dora and Em'ly, I noticed how beautiful she was. Eventually I told her, "I went away, dear Agnes, loving you. I stayed away, loving you. I returned home, loving you." She laid her gentle hands on my shoulders and looked at me calmly. "I have loved you all my life," she said.

OLIVER TWIST

In a workhouse, in an unnamed English town, a child was born into a world of sorrow. His young, unmarried mother died before she could give him a name or tell anyone hers. Named by the authorities, Oliver Twist was sent to the parish baby farm to endure nine years of hunger and harshness until Mr. Bumble, the parish beadle, returned him to the workhouse.

Food was scarce in the workhouse, and when Oliver asked bravely, "Please Sir, I want some more," he was punished severely.

Five pounds was offered to anyone who would take Oliver as an apprentice. Cruel Mr. Gamfield, the chimney sweep, applied but was rejected when the half-blind magistrate noticed Oliver's terror.

Eventually, Oliver was apprenticed to Mr. Sowerberry, the undertaker. There he met cruel Noah Claypole and the servant girl Charlotte, who was in love with Noah. Oliver was fed with cold bits put by for the dog. Worse still was his nightly feeling of awe and dread—for he had to sleep amongst the unfinished coffins.

Oliver had to work as a mourner. His pale, melancholy face proved especially useful for children's funerals. Noah was a bully and said cruel things about Oliver's mother. A fight began, causing Mrs. Sowerberry to lock Oliver in the coal cellar and send Noah for Mr. Bumble. "It's not Madness, ma'am ... it's Meat," claimed Mr. Bumble, implying that Oliver was being treated too well.

Upset and angry, Oliver ran away. As he passed the workhouse, he met a dying child called Dick. "God bless you," said the poor boy—the first good wishes Oliver had ever received.

Workhouses were places where the poor did unpaid work in exchange for food and accommodation. There, conditions were harsh, and families were often split up.

Arriving in London, exhausted and penniless, Oliver met another boy—the roistering, swaggering Artful Dodger, who took him to an old man called Fagin who seemed to have care of several boys. Warm, well fed and lulled by hot gin and water, Oliver slept deeply. He awoke to see Fagin gloating over a secret hoard of treasure. Noticing Oliver was awake, Fagin grabbed a knife as if to silence the boy for ever. Luckily, the old man calmed down. Later, Fagin taught his boys to pick pockets.

After much practice, Oliver was sent out with Charlie and Dodger, who picked the pocket of a gentleman reading at a book stall. Shocked, Oliver ran. The gentleman missed his handkerchief and cried, "Stop thief!" A chase began, in which Charlie and Dodger gleefully took part! Oliver was knocked down, but the gentleman took pity on him and went with him to the police station.

Oliver was locked in a filthy cell. Mr. Brownlow, the gentleman, felt that he had seen Oliver before but he could not recall where.

When Oliver was brought before the rude and incompetent magistrate Fang, he was too afraid to speak. Just in time, the bookseller rushed in, saying that Oliver was not the thief. So it was that Oliver went home with Mr. Brownlow and was cared for by his kindly housekeeper, Mrs. Bedwin. The boy became fascinated by a portrait hanging in his bedroom. Mr. Brownlow was amazed to see the likeness between Oliver and the woman in the portrait.

Fagin and his friend Bill Sikes, who made his living robbing houses, discussed recapturing Oliver—Bill's girlfriend Nancy was at the magistrate's office and observed the trial.

Back at Mr. Brownlow's, the portrait had been removed, and Oliver was happy. When Mr. Brownlow had books to be returned to the bookseller, Oliver begged, "Do let me take them! I'll run all the way."

In Clerkenwell, Oliver turned down a by-street and was grabbed by Nancy. A crowd gathered. "Thank gracious goodness heavins, I've found him!" cried Nancy, claiming Oliver as her brother.

*In Victorian times, many working-class people could not read or write. A **book stall** would be a good place to find well-to-do people with pockets ripe for picking.*

Returned to Fagin and Sikes, Oliver feared Mr. Brownlow would think him a thief, but the gang just laughed. Oliver tried to run, and was saved from being savaged by Sikes's dog when Nancy screamed, "Keep back the dog ... the child shan't be torn down by the dog unless you kill me first."

Oliver was caught, but Nancy grabbed the club with which Fagin began to beat him. The brutal Sikes wrestled with Nancy until she passed out.

Mr. Brownlow did not forget Oliver. On a visit to London, Mr. Bumble the beadle spied a newspaper advertisement offering five guineas for information about Oliver Twist. He called on Mr. Brownlow and told many lies about Oliver.

Meanwhile, Fagin and Sikes decided Oliver should help with a robbery. On a cold, rainy morning, Oliver and Sikes trudged west through London to meet Toby Crackit and Barney. Oliver was lifted through the small window of an elegant house. He meant to raise the alarm, but two servants appeared inside and Oliver was shot. Sikes dragged him back through the window, and they ran.

Back at the workhouse, Mr. Bumble was about to propose to Mrs. Corney, the workhouse matron, when she was summoned to the deathbed of Old Sally, who tended Oliver's mother when she died. Sally confessed that Oliver's mother had saved some gold with which to buy him some "friends". "I robbed her, so I did. She wasn't cold—I tell you she wasn't cold, when I stole it," cried Sally.

Back at Fagin's house, Toby Crackit returned from the failed robbery. When Fagin learned that Sikes had abandoned Oliver in a ditch, he rushed to the Three Cripples tavern. Barney had not returned either.

Fagin found Nancy, who appeared to have been drinking heavily. He raged about Oliver being worth hundreds of pounds. Nancy pretended not to understand, saying Oliver was "better where he is, than among us."

Fagin went home, where he found a man waiting for him. This nervous character was called Monks and appeared to have an interest in the fate of Oliver Twist. It seemed that he wanted the boy to be out of the way but did not wish him dead.

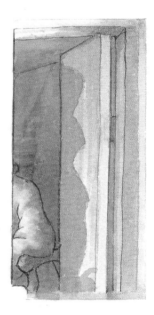

In Dickens' lifetime **drunkenness** *was a problem for men and women. Throughout London's slums, gin and ale were cheap and readily available.*

As day dawned, Oliver climbed from his ditch with a cry of pain. His left arm, bandaged in a shawl, hung useless at his side. The shawl was saturated with blood.

The desperate boy staggered towards a house, only to faint on the doorstep. It was the house of the robbery, and the servants recognized Oliver, but Mrs. Maylie and her niece Rose, who lived there, were kind to him.

Beautiful Rose Maylie was seventeen. She insisted that Oliver should be carried up to bed and that Dr. Losberne should be summoned.

Later that day Oliver told his story. Convinced of his innocence, Dr. Losberne persuaded the servant Giles that the thief he shot was not Oliver. Just then, the Bow Street Runners arrived, but they were unable to solve the crime. When Oliver felt better, Dr. Losberne took him to see Mr. Brownlow. On the way, Oliver recognized the house where the robbers met before the robbery. Dr. Losberne spoke to a man there, asking for Sikes by name. He left without success, but not before the man had caught a glimpse of Oliver.

The Bow Street Runners *were a semi-official group organized in the mid-eighteenth century. Their primary role was finding and arresting robbers. In 1839, they were replaced by a professional police force.*

When Oliver and Dr. Losberne arrived back in London, they found that Mr. Brownlow had left for the West Indies.

With continued kindness, the Maylies took Oliver with them when they moved into the countryside. In this idyllic setting, however, Rose fell ill and Oliver was asked to send a letter summoning Dr. Losberne. On his way home, Oliver had a disturbing encounter with a man who looked into his eyes and cried, "Death!"

Fortunately, Rose recovered. Mrs. Maylie's son Henry arrived, declaring his love for Rose, but Mrs. Maylie feared that "youth has many generous impulses which do not last."

Henry, who was running for parliament with the help of his powerful uncle, asked Rose to marry him. Rose feared that her past would hinder his career and so refused. When Henry left, he asked Oliver to write to him every fortnight.

Sitting over his books one night, Oliver awoke from a nightmare to see Fagin at the window. With him was the man who had cried, "Death!" Oliver raised the alarm, but, though they searched, the Maylie household could find no evidence of Fagin's visit.

*A **pawnbroker** is a person who lends money. Personal property of a similar value is left as security. The property can be sold if the loan and interest are not repaid within the specified time.*

Back at the workhouse, Mr. Bumble met Monks in a tavern and, in a crumbling building by a river, Mrs. Bumble made Monks pay twenty-five sovereigns before she would speak of Oliver's origins.

She described how, when Old Sally died, she took the pawnbroker's ticket out of her hand and redeemed a beautiful gold locket containing two hairs and a wedding ring engraved with "Agnes" and a date within a year of Oliver's birth. Monks took the jewellery and, opening a trapdoor, dropped them into the raging river below.

Later, as Fagin and Monks whispered together, Nancy eavesdropped. Shocked by what she heard, she drugged Sikes with laudanum and went to see Rose.

Nancy told Rose that Monks knew of Oliver's parentage and destroyed the evidence to be sure he got an inheritance—for Monks was Oliver's half-brother. Refusing money from Rose, Nancy hurried home, terrified that Sikes would have discovered her missing.

The following day, Rose, Mrs. Maylie, Henry, Mr. Brownlow, and Dr. Losberne decided to secure Oliver his inheritance.

Nancy tried to meet Rose once more, this time on London Bridge. Fagin was suspicious and had Nancy followed. When Sikes was told of what he saw as Nancy's treachery, he rushed home and beat his pistol on her upturned face. Almost blind with blood, Nancy held Rose's white handkerchief to heaven, praying for mercy. Sikes murdered her with a club—even his dog's paws became bloody.

Confronted by Mr. Brownlow, Monks revealed himself to be Edward Leeford, the son of Mr. Brownlow's oldest friend. This friend was forced into an unhappy marriage, which produced Monks. Later he met Agnes, whom he hoped to marry, but he died while she was pregnant. No will was found, so his estate went to his first wife.

When Mr. Brownlow first rescued Oliver, he had no idea of his identity. It was the picture of Agnes left by his friend that gave him a clue.

Two days later, Oliver went back to his birthplace, where he met his half-brother Monks. When Mr. Leeford died, Monks's mother had destroyed the letter he left for Agnes, Oliver's mother, explaining he was already married—albeit unhappily. Monks's mother had also destroyed the will naming Oliver as heir. The discovery was made that Rose was Oliver's mother's younger sister, the boy's aunt.

Unfortunately for Oliver, his dear friend Dick had died, but with the mysteries all solved, the Bumbles lost their jobs and, though Monks escaped from England, he died in a New World prison. Sikes, too, met his death as he tried to escape across the rooftops. Henry Maylie, now a curate, married Rose at last. As befit someone so evil, Fagin was tried and condemned to hang, while Oliver lived happily and peacefully amongst his friends in the countryside.

THE OLD CURIOSITY SHOP

While walking through the dark streets of London one night, taking pleasure in speculating about the people he saw around him, an infirm old man was approached by a pretty little girl who was lost. Her name was Nell Trent. The old man, whose name was Master Humphrey, helped her back to her home, which turned out to be a shop filled with old and curious things: suits of armour, fantastic carvings, rusty weapons, furniture, and figures in china, wood, iron and ivory.

At the strange shop, Master Humphrey met Nell's grandfather, who clearly adored her. He also made the acquaintance of Kit Nubbles, an honest lad equally devoted to the little girl. As Master Humphrey left, Nell's grandfather also went out into the night.

A week later, the old man returned to the shop. Interrupting a boisterous debate inside, he found Nell's brother Fred and Fred's friend Richard Swiveller. Nell was out but soon arrived with one

Daniel Quilp, a short, elderly man with restless, sly eyes and an unwholesome complexion. Quilp lived at Tower Hill, where his wife and his mother-in-law, Mrs. Jiniwin, suffered cruelly at his hands.

One day, Nell took a letter from her grandfather to Quilp at his wharf. Quilp seemed perplexed by its contents and frightened Nell by suggesting that she should become "Mrs. Quilp the second, when Mrs. Quilp the first is dead".

*A **wharf** is a sturdy platform built by the side of a harbour or river. It is used for the loading and unloading of boats and for the storage of goods.*

Quilp took Nell back to his home and listened behind the door while the girl confided to Mrs. Quilp that her grandfather went out of the house each night. Nell explained that her beloved grandfather seemed like a different person now. "We were once so happy and he so cheerful and contented!" she said in distress. "You cannot think what a sad change has fallen on us, since."

Quilp was not the only one to have designs on Little Nell. At Fred's lodgings, he and Richard discussed Richard marrying her. They believed her grandfather was rich and wanted a share of the fortune.

Just three nights after Nell's confession to Mrs. Quilp, her grandfather, who had been ill all day, said he would not be going out that night. Suddenly, Quilp appeared, crying, "You have no secret from me now." He had discovered that Nell's grandfather had been gambling and claimed it was the faithful Kit who told him.

In fact, Kit was at his usual post, standing in the shadow of an archway in the street outside and keeping a watch over the comings and goings at the shop until Little Nell was safely in bed.

Daniel Quilp's evil actions were not without consequences for Kit. When he was back at his home, Nell arrived with some money. Her grandfather, she said, had had some kind of fit and discharged Kit from his service. "He complains and raves of you," said Nell.

Now the coast was clear, Quilp and his lawyer, Sampson Brass, took up residence in the curiosity shop. But Kit was worried about Nell and took every opportunity to try to see her, often being turned away from the door. Eventually, he managed to have a word and offered her the front room upstairs in his house as a refuge. "Mother says it would be just the thing for you," he said.

Quilp's plans were foiled, however, when, on a June morning, Nell stole the key from Quilp and escaped with her grandfather. They had nowhere to go and became beggars.

Nell was particularly sad to leave her pet bird, a linnet, behind. After she left, Kit fought Tom, Quilp's wharf boy, for the bird.

Searching for work, Kit Nubbles met a Mr. and Mrs. Garland on their way to see Mr. Witherden, the notary. They had no change, so gave Kit a shilling for holding their horse, when the usual rate was sixpence (half a shilling).

Punch and Judy *was (and still is) a puppet show that probably originated in Italy. Although it is usually seen as a children's entertainment, the show is very violent, with Punch attacking his wife and baby.*

In a nearby graveyard, Nell and her grandfather met Short Trotters and Tommy Codlin the Punch men. "Look," said Tommy, "here's Judy's clothes falling to pieces again. You haven't got a needle and thread, I suppose?" Nell helped to mend Judy and secretly sewed a gold coin into her own dress. Nell and the old man travelled with the Punch men, but by the time they reached the races, Nell was feeling uneasy. While a show was in progress, the pair made their escape.

In Victorian times, a **notary** *was an official authorized to prepare legal documents. He also had the power to administer oaths.*

When Nell had been gone a week, Kit was still hopeful she would soon return. He went to the notary to work off the other half of his shilling, and ended up being hired by Mr. and Mrs. Garland of Abel Cottage, Finchley. Here he met a servant-girl called Barbara.

Meanwhile, Quilp and Richard Swiveller went together to the Wilderness tavern, and the evil Quilp agreed to help Richard marry Nell, knowing that her grandfather had no fortune.

Nell and her grandfather had been lucky to meet and stay with a kindly schoolmaster. Next day he said, "You're very welcome to pass another night here. I should be really glad if you would." It so happened that while the visitors were there, the schoolmaster's favourite pupil died.

Nell and her grandfather continued their journey, joining up with Mrs. Jarley and George, who owned a travelling waxworks show. Nell secured a job showing visitors around the waxworks. One evening, Nell caught sight of Quilp, but luckily he did not see her. Later, out for a walk, she and her grandfather were caught in a violent storm. As they sheltered at the Valiant Soldier tavern, Nell's grandfather began to gamble, losing everything that was left in Nell's purse.

They stayed the night, paying with the coin sewn into Nell's dress. While the distressed girl was in bed, a creature entered her room. Silently and stealthily, it stole the change from the coin. The robber was her grandfather, but next morning Nell could not get

him to confess. At the waxworks once more, Nell's grandfather went out late at night and returned penniless but still determined to gamble. He believed he must do it to secure Nell's future.

Back in London, Quilp persuaded Sampson Brass and his sister Sally to take on Richard Swiveller as a clerk. Richard was alone in the office when a little voice from very low down said, "Oh please, will you come and show the lodgings?" It was a servant-girl in a coarse, dirty apron. Shown the lodgings, a single gentleman brought up his trunk, paid and went to bed in the middle of the day. It was impossible to wake him. The new lodger later revealed a special interest in Punch shows, eventually meeting Short Trotters and Tommy Codlin. He gave them each a sovereign, promising if Nell was found, it was "but a prelude to twenty more".

On the quarter day, Kit and Barbara got a half-day holiday and so gathered with their mothers and Kit's two younger brothers for tea at Kit's mother's house. They watched a play and ate oysters. To Barbara's annoyance, Kit spoke repeatedly of Nell's beauty.

Next day, Kit had to go to the notary's—the mysterious lodger had found Nell. Afraid to upset his old master, Kit refused to go but suggested his mother went instead.

Far away, Nell's grandfather was still gambling. Nell observed him with some gypsies, who suggested he stole the waxwork takings. Nell told him she had had a terrible dream. "I have had it once before," she said. "It is a dream of grey-haired men like you, in darkened rooms by night, robbing sleepers of their gold. Up! ... Nothing but flight can save us."

Arriving in a filthy, industrial town, Nell and her grandfather were helped by a stranger, miserably clad and begrimed with smoke. He took them to a foundry, where they were able to sleep on a heap of warm ashes. Next day, their money ran out. "Charity! A morsel of bread!" begged Nell, but the people had nothing to give. She fainted from weakness.

The schoolmaster, who was travelling to a new employer, carried Nell to an inn and summoned a doctor. When she had recovered, Nell and her grandfather went with the schoolmaster by stage wagon to a peaceful, country place.

By the time Kit's mother and the gentleman lodger reached the waxworks, Nell was not there. In an inn, Kit's mother and the gentleman met Quilp.

Dissatisfied, the parties returned home, but while Kit welcomed his mother with open arms, Quilp arrived to find his wife, his mother-in-law and Sampson Brass drinking his spirits in the belief that he was dead. Only Tom the wharf boy was pleased to see him.

Nell, her grandfather and the schoolmaster arrived at their destination, a village with thatched cottages, a stream and the blue Welsh mountains just visible far away. Here they met the clergyman, and Nell was employed to caretake the church.

Back in London, whenever Kit brought a message, Sampson Brass sent Richard on an errand and gave Kit some money, saying it was from the gentleman lodger. One day, Richard went downstairs and played cards with the small servant, whom he liked and named "the Marchioness".

When Sally claimed a silver pencilcase and a knife were missing, Sampson said he was also missing some money. He placed a five-pound note on his desk. Kit arrived, and Sampson insisted he put down his hat. As Sampson was speaking, he moved the hat once or twice. Then he asked, "Will you mind the office one minute, while I run upstairs?" Later, the note was found in Kit's hat. He was arrested.

Quilp made Sampson fire Richard. Shortly afterwards, Richard developed a raging fever. The small servant girl escaped the Brass household and for three weeks tenderly nursed him. When he recovered, he asked her, "What has become of Kit?" Afraid to make him ill again, the girl told how she overheard Sampson and Sally plotting to put the money in Kit's hat. The cowardly Sampson was tricked into confessing his evil deeds, but Sally slipped quietly away. She sent a note warning Quilp, who, trying to escape from the wharf in thick fog, stumbled into the water and was drowned.

*A **sexton** was a man employed to take care of a church. His role was a varied one, often including digging graves and bell-ringing.*

At a reception held to celebrate Kit's release, Mr. Garland revealed that his brother was a friend of the clergyman in the country. Mr. Garland, Kit and the gentleman lodger set off through the snow to find Nell. During the journey, the gentleman revealed that he was the younger brother of Nell's grandfather. Arriving after midnight, they had to wake the sexton and ask him to point out the right house.

Kit opened a door to see a man sitting with bowed head by the dull, red glow of a fire. No lamp or candle was lit. Kit recognized his old master. The visitors gently approached Nell, lying on her bed. Hoping to please her, Kit had brought the linnet. However, although her grandfather was too confused to know it, Nell was not asleep. She was dead, having passed away two days before.

A local child took Nell's grandfather for a walk while Nell was being buried. The vault was covered, and the stone fixed down. When the old man returned, he searched in vain, calling pitifully for Nell. When told she was dead, he fell down like a murdered man. There seemed little chance of him surviving, but eventually he pulled through. He began to go each day to wait for Nell at her grave. On a genial day in spring he was found dead on her stone, and was laid in the earth by her side.

With Nell and her grandfather both dead, Sampson Brass was found guilty of numerous crimes. However, because he co-operated with the police, he escaped transportation and was merely imprisoned. Some rumours said that his sister became a sailor, some said a soldier who could be seen standing to attention in St. James's Park. Many believed that both Sampson and Sally ended up as vagrants.

Daniel Quilp's body was recovered and a verdict of suicide returned. Only Tom the wharf boy cried at the inquest. Mrs. Quilp remarried and set out to enjoy her first husband's money. The Garlands continued to live at Abel Cottage.

Unfortunately, Nell's brother Fred drowned in France. Having been left an annual allowance in his rich aunt's will, Richard Swiveller educated and then married the Marchioness. The schoolmaster stayed in his idyllic country spot, and the gentleman lodger, although filled with sadness by the course that events had taken, took great delight in retracing the steps of Nell and her grandfather and being kind to those who had been kind to them.

Kit found a new position, and his mother and brothers were secured from want and made quite happy. Kit did not remain a single man all his life but eventually married Barbara. Together they had children of their own, much to the delight of both mothers, and often Kit gathered them to him and told them of good Miss Nell who died. When they cried to hear the tale of woe, he reminded them that she had gone to heaven and that they would go there too if they were good. In heaven he assured them, everyone would be happy, and they would know Nell as he had done as a boy.

Sometimes he took the little ones to the street where Nell had lived. However, time had passed, and the house that once held all the old curious things, the suits of armour, fantastic carvings, rusty weapons, furniture, figures in china, iron and ivory, had been pulled down. Soon Kit could no longer be certain of the spot where the shop had stood.

Such are the changes that a few years bring about, and so do things pass away, like a tale that is told…

NICHOLAS NICKLEBY

Ralph Nickleby lived in Golden Square, London. His neighbours believed him rich, though none quite knew how he earned his money. He had cold, restless eyes.

One day, as he was returning home from a meeting, Ralph was met by Newman Noggs, his assistant, a tall man of middle age with a false eye. He handed Ralph an envelope edged in black—Ralph's brother had died, leaving his family penniless. Not at all upset, Ralph called on his brother's widow and her children, called Nicholas and Kate. They had travelled up from Devon and were lodging at the house of Miss La Creevy in the Strand.

Appealed to for help, Ralph Nickleby showed Nicholas an advertisement for an assistant at Mr. Wackford Squeers' school, Dotheboys Hall, in Yorkshire, claiming "let him get that situation and his fortune is made." Hesitant at first, Nicholas eventually replied, "I am ready to do anything you wish me. Let us try our fortune with Mr. Squeers at once."

*A **trunk** is a large, strong box, used when travelling. It might contain clothes or books. A deal trunk was an inexpensive one made of planks of pine.*

Near Smithfield Market was the Saracen's Head Inn. At half past three one afternoon, a small, unhappy looking boy was sitting on a deal trunk in the Coffee Room. By him was Mr. Wackford Squeers, dressed in a suit of scholastic black. He had but one eye, and the blank side of his face was much wrinkled. His appearance was sinister, especially when he smiled. As he was speaking to Mr. Snawley, who was considering sending his two stepsons to Dotheboys, Ralph entered, offering the services of his nephew Nicholas, "hot from school, with everything he learned there fermenting in his head, and nothing fermenting in his pocket," Squeers considered, then turned to Nicholas, who had accompanied his uncle, and said, "Your uncle's recommendation has done it." Nicholas was hired.

Ralph sent Nicholas home to pack, giving him some documents and saying, "Leave these papers with my clerk."

In Golden Square, Newman Noggs turned very pale when Nicholas announced he was going to Dotheboys. Nicholas's gentle sister Kate had her doubts as well. When she met Mr. Squeers, she asked her brother, "What kind of place can it be that you are going to?" But Nicholas was decided.

As he climbed into the stagecoach that would take him to the school, Nicholas called to his mother, "Bless you, love, and goodbye." When no one was looking, Newman Noggs secretly handed the young man a note, mysteriously whispering, "Take it. Read it. Nobody knows."

Nicholas travelled with Mr. Squeers and some boys on their way to become pupils at Dotheboys. The journey to Yorkshire was harsh, but eventually they arrived at a long, cold-looking house, one storey high, with a few straggling outbuildings behind. A strange, tall boy, whom Nicholas learnt was named Smike, opened the yard gate and stepped forward with a lamp.

Later, Nicholas ate a frugal supper with Mr. and Mrs. Squeers and soon met their daughter Fanny and their son Wackford.

Miniatures are very small, intricate paintings. During the Victorian period, portraits in this style were immensely popular, painted in oils or watercolours.

That night, as he prepared for bed, Nicholas opened the letter from Newman. Because Nicholas's father had once helped him, Newman was offering assistance to Nicholas, should he ever need it.

Back in London, Kate was sitting for Miss La Creevy, who painted miniatures, when Ralph arrived. He had found work for Kate with the milliner Madame Mantalini. Though not the position she had hoped for, Kate said, "I am very much obliged to you, uncle."

Ralph had also arranged new lodgings for his relatives. Newman took Kate and Mrs. Nickleby to rooms in a dingy house in Thames Street. "This house depresses and chills one," shivered Kate, "as if some blight had fallen on it."

Although poor himself, Newman Noggs had done his best, organizing some furniture, milk for tea, and coal for the women.

Unaware of all this, Nicholas was learning the full horrors of Dotheboys Hall. The schoolroom was bare and dirty, its broken windows stopped up with old copybooks. The ill-treated pupils were thin, with the faces of old men darkened by suffering and neglect. When Smike asked, "is the world as bad and dismal as this place?" Nicholas Nickleby replied, "its hardest, coarsest toil were happiness to this."

Having fallen in love with Nicholas, Fanny Squeers arranged a tea party, where Nicholas met Fanny's friend Matilda and Matilda's fiancé, the large Yorkshireman John Browdie. Nicholas's feelings were confused, but he later told Fanny that he had "not one thought wish or hope" of affection for her. Fanny was very distressed by this declaration.

The miserable life at Dotheboys Hall continued. One freezing January morning, Smike was found to be missing. Mr. and Mrs. Squeers scoured the countryside until he was recaptured. With the whole school assembled, Mr. Squeers began to beat Smike.

"Stop!" cried Nicholas in a voice that made the rafters ring. "This must not go on."

Aghast, Squeers released Smike. Then, in a violent outbreak of wrath and with a cry like the howl of a wild beast, Squeers spat at Nicholas and struck him across the face. Concentrating all his feelings of rage, scorn and indignation, Nicholas sprang upon Squeers, wrestling the cane from his hand and grabbing him by the throat before beating the ruffian until he roared for mercy.

Nicholas left the school on foot. On the way, he met John Browdie, who congratulated him on what he had done. Next morning he awoke in a barn. Smike, who had followed him, dropped to his knees, begging, "take me with you, pray." "Come," said Nicholas.

Newman Noggs was with his friends the Kenwigs when Nicholas and Smike arrived from Yorkshire, exhausted. A letter had already been sent from Fanny Squeers to Ralph, but luckily Ralph was away.

Staying with Newman but in urgent need of work, Nicholas went to the General Agency Office, where he saw a pretty girl, neatly attired, accompanied by a slovenly, red-faced girl. He refused work with a corrupt MP.

Unaware that Nicholas was in London, Kate was unhappy working at Madame Mantalini's. One evening Ralph invited her to supper at his

A *General Agency Office* was a place where employers could advertise for servants such as cooks, butlers, secretaries or parlour maids, and people with skills to offer could advertise for work. Today it might be called an Employment Agency.

house, saying, "Come in a hackney coach. I'll pay. Good night … a … a … God bless you." Somehow the blessing seemed to stick in his throat. Mrs. Nickleby was excited about her daughter's invitation, so Kate was ready in her black silk dress long before the ordered carriage arrived.

At Golden Square, Ralph took his niece into an opulent room where some gentlemen were gathered. They were introduced to her as Mr. Pluck, Mr. Pyke, Sir Mulberry Hawk and Lord Frederick Verisopht, who said, "devilish pretty" on sight of her.

At dinner, Kate had to sit between Lord Frederick and Sir Mulberry. When Sir Mulberry behaved cruelly, Kate rushed out. Sir Mulberry followed her upstairs. When Kate attempted to escape, he grabbed her dress. "Unhand me, sir, this instant!" cried Kate. "Not for the world!" was the aristocrat's evil reply.

"What is this?" demanded Ralph, appearing in the doorway. Taking Sir Mulberry to one side, Ralph confessed, "As a matter of business I thought she might make some impression on the silly youth…. I thought to draw him on more gently by this device." Ralph, it seemed, was a money-lender, and Kate was part of his plan to entrap Lord Frederick.

Kate took time to recover from her ordeal and was with her mother when Ralph arrived with Fanny's letter about Nicholas, which was packed with slanderous exaggerations. Kate cried indignantly, "It is some base conspiracy!" "Everything combines to prove the truth," insisted Ralph.

"A lie!" roared a voice outside. The door was dashed open and Nicholas entered. Furious, he decided he must leave London. Taking his leave of his mother and sister, he told Ralph, "There will be a day of reckoning sooner or later, and it will be a heavy one for you if they are wronged."

Smike and Nicholas travelled to Portsmouth, where they met a certain Mr. Vincent Crummles and surprisingly became successful provincial actors.

In London, the bailiffs arrived at Madame Mantalini's shop. In need of new employment, Kate became a companion to the insipid Mrs. Witterly in Cadogan Place.

Meanwhile, Lord Frederick and Sir Mulberry hatched a plot regarding Kate. They met Mrs. Nickleby at Ralph's office and escorted her home. The attentions of the two noblemen made Kate's life so distressing that she pleaded with her uncle to intervene—to no avail.

In Victorian times, **companies of actors** *would travel from town to town. Before the days of cinema and television, their performances were a popular source of entertainment.*

Newman Noggs overheard Kate's pleas. "Don't cry any more," he whispered, "I shall see you soon. Ha! ha! ha! And so shall somebody else too." He immediately wrote to Nicholas, who set off back to London with Smike.

When Nicholas and Smike stopped for refreshment in a hotel, Nicholas overheard a man referring to "little Kate Nickleby". It was Sir Mulberry out with Lord Frederick. "Your name and address?" demanded Nicholas, keen to defend his sister's honour. When Sir Mulberry refused to give either, Nicholas climbed on to his carriage. Sir Mulberry thrashed Nicholas with his whip, but Nicholas grabbed the handle and sliced his antagonist's face. As the horse bolted, Nicholas was thrown free. Further up the street, the carriage crashed.

Nicholas at once went to Newman, who explained what Kate had been enduring. While Nicholas moved his family from Thames Street, Newman secretly delivered a note from Nicholas to Ralph: "Your kindred renounce you, for they know no shame but the ties of blood which bind them in name with you."

Luckily, Nicholas met Ned and Charles Cheeryble, who employed him as a clerk. One day, Nicholas entered Charles's room to find the pretty girl from the General Agency Office on her knees and in distress. Shocked, he retreated.

Just as things were going better for Nicholas and his family and friends, Smike was captured by Squeers, who locked him in a room at Mr. Snawley's house. Only thanks to John Browdie, who was visiting London with his new wife Matilda, was Smike rescued.

Out collecting interest payments from those to whom he had lent money, Ralph met a poverty-stricken man. Twenty years ago this man, Brooker, used to be his clerk, but Ralph treated him badly and they fell out. "Are those of your name dear to you?" Brooker asked threateningly, when Ralph refused to give him money. "They are not," was Ralph's reply.

John and Matilda were taking tea with Mrs. Nickleby when Ralph entered with Squeers and Mr. Snawley. "I have his father here," claimed Ralph, pointing to Smike. "I want my son," demanded Mr. Snawley. Terrified, Smike cried, "I will not go from you with him." Official-looking papers were produced, but Nicholas suspected a cunning trick and Smike stayed.

One day, Charles Cheeryble asked Nicholas if he would help him assist the young woman from the General Agency Office without her father knowing. The young woman was called Madeline Bray and was the daughter of a woman, now dead, whom Charles had loved in his youth. Nicholas agreed.

Meanwhile, Newman Noggs overheard another money-lender, named Gride, telling Ralph about his plans to marry Madeline in return for cancelling a debt. Because Mr. Bray was also in debt to Ralph, Gride needed Ralph's help. Newman told Nicholas what he had heard, and the young man pleaded with Madeline not to go ahead with the wedding—to no avail. He even offered Gride money but was refused.

*A **will** is a legal document. It says what a person wants to happen to their property and their money after their death. A **beneficiary** is someone who gains from the will.*

On the morning of the wedding, Nicholas went to the Brays' house with Kate. While he was arguing with Gride and Ralph, the thud of something falling was heard above. Madeline screamed. Her father had dropped dead. Though Gride and Ralph protested, Nicholas carried Madeline to a carriage and took her to stay with his mother.

Gride's housekeeper, the deaf Mrs. Sliderskew, soon went missing with some important papers. Squeers was persuaded by Ralph to assist in their recovery. After a clever surveillance operation, Newman Noggs and the Cheeryble brothers' nephew Frank apprehended Squeers and Mrs. Sliderskew with the stolen papers. One of the papers found tucked inside Squeers' coat was the will of Madeline Bray's maternal grandfather. Madeline was the beneficiary.

In an effort to restore Smike's failing health, Nicholas took him to Devon. Resting in the garden, Smike was shocked to catch a glimpse of the man who first took him to Dotheboys Hall. Soon afterwards, Smike died.

Things were going from bad to worse for Ralph Nickleby. His associates deserted him, and a bad deal lost him ten thousand pounds. He then learnt from Brooker that, many years ago, when Ralph's estranged wife died, Brooker lied about the fate of Ralph's son. The child did not die but was taken by Brooker to Dotheboys. Said Brooker, "I was confirmed in my design of opening up the secret one day, and making it a means of getting money." Now it was too late—Smike was Ralph's son. As rain and hail pattered against the window, Ralph took his own life.

For others, there was a happier ending. Nicholas married Madeline, and Kate married the Cheeryble brothers' nephew Frank. Mrs. Nickleby lived sometimes with her son and sometimes with her daughter. Close to Nicholas lived faithful Newman Noggs.

Up in Yorkshire, "Squeers is in prison, and we are going to run away!" cried a score of shrill voices. Such a cheer rose as the walls of Dotheboys Hall had never heard. As the sound faded, not a boy was left in the school.